Kitten Friends #2

Bob the Bouncy Kitten

by Jenny Dale

illustrated by Susan Hellard

Aladdin Paperbacks

New York   London   Toronto   Sydney   Singapore

Look for these KITTEN FRIENDS books!

Special thanks to Mary Hooper
To Lily—who also likes to leap up curtains!

First Aladdin Paperbacks edition October 2000
Text copyright © 1999 by Working Partners Limited
Illustrations copyright © 1999 by Susan Hellard
First published 1999 by Macmillan Children's Books U.K.
Created by Working Partners Limited

Aladdin Paperbacks
An imprint of Simon & Schuster Children's Publishing
1230 Avenue of the Americas
New York, NY 10020

The text for this book was set in 16-point Palatino
Printed and bound in the United States of America
2 4 6 8 10 9 7 5 3 1

Library of Congress Catalog Card Number: 00-107110

ISBN 0-689-84109-4

Chapter One

"Got you, Bob!" yelled Amy Myers, lifting her kitten from his hiding place behind the ironing board.

"At last!" Amy's mother sighed. She picked up the cat basket and opened the lid. "Come on, Bob! It's for your own good," she said.

For twenty minutes Amy and Mrs. Myers had been chasing Bob, Amy's kitten, around the house. It was time for him to visit the vet for his second flu shot. But Bob didn't want to be shut inside the basket. They'd chased him up and down the stairs, in and out of the bedrooms—all over the place!

"In you go, Bob," Amy said. She lowered the wriggling ginger bundle into the basket. Bob twitched and squirmed and made meowing noises of protest. "Shut the lid, Mom!"

From the basket, Bob looked up at them, his eyes dark and wide. Then, just as the lid was almost closed, he made a leap for freedom. Squeezing himself out of a tiny opening, he bounced onto the carpet and raced across the room.

"Oh, no!" Amy cried.

"The little devil!" said her mother, annoyed. She put the basket down. "I've got work to do, Amy," she said. "I can't waste any more time. I suggest you get him in the basket and tell me when you've done it. Then I'll drive you to the vet." She went upstairs to her office.

Amy sat on the floor and sighed. She could just see the point of Bob's ginger tail sticking out from under a cushion on the sofa. "You're a little terror," she said to him. She didn't mean it, though. Bob was gorgeous, and she loved him to pieces. He had soft, gingery fur with just a smudge of white under his chin and another on his squishy tummy. And he had soft, pink paws—very soft, because he'd never been outside—and glinty green eyes. But Bob was also the friskiest, bounciest kitten she had ever seen!

Bob was Amy's first pet. She'd had him just four weeks, and because it was the summer holidays, she'd been with him nearly every moment of that time. She had photographs of him all over her bedroom wall, on the table next to her bed, and stuck inside her diary. And you could just guess what the subject of her school summer project was. . . .

Keeping an eye on the scrap of Bob's tail that she could see, Amy sat down on the floor and yawned. She'd been awake at five o'clock that morning. Bob had woken her up by bouncing onto the bed and licking her nose. When she hadn't said hello to him right away, he'd gone down to the bottom of the bed and tunneled under the covers to play with her toes.

Amy had an idea. She stretched and

yawned noisily, then curled up on the floor and pretended to go to sleep. But she kept one eye half open, to see what Bob would do.

After a couple of minutes, Bob came out from behind the cushion and made his way toward her, whiskers quivering,

one dainty paw in front of the other.

Amy kept still as Bob stepped gently onto her leg. Then, suddenly, in one swift movement, she scooped him up. "Got you!" she said to the surprised kitten. Quick as a flash, she plonked him inside the open basket and shut the lid.

Bob meowed indignantly.

"Got you good, this time," Amy said, smiling. She fastened the catch and carried the basket into the hall. "I've got him, Mom!" she called up the stairway. "Can we go now?"

"He's a fine, healthy kitten," the vet said, putting Bob back into this basket after his shot. And now that he's had his second shot, he can go outside." She smiled at Amy. "Bob may be a bit groggy after this shot, so let him take it easy for the rest of the day. But you can take him out to play in the backyard tomorrow."

Amy nodded happily. She could hardly wait. She and Bob were going to have so much fun!

"That's good," Amy's mother said. "I hope that means Bob will be a little quieter in the house once he's run around outside. At the moment he races around like a whirlwind!"

"I bet he'll calm down as he gets older," said the vet.

Amy and her mother left the vet's

office with Bob. Driving home, there wasn't a squeak or meow from Bob. He just lay quietly at the bottom of his basket.

"I hope he's not feeling bad," Amy said anxiously,

When they reached home, she carried the basket indoors, taking care not to bang it against anything. Still, everything was quiet in the basket.

"Do you think Bob's okay?" Amy asked her mother worriedly. "He didn't react like this after his first shot."

Mrs. Myers shrugged. "Maybe this one was stronger," she suggested.

Amy opened the lid of the basket, ready to lift her fluffy kitten out. But as she did so, Bob shot out of the basket so fast, he was a blur.

He leaped onto the arm of the sofa and bounced up to the windowsill. "Fooled you!" he meowed. Then he scampered up the curtains to sit on the curtain rod. He looked down at Amy and her mother, his green eyes shining. "Feeling bad, did you say?" said Mrs. Myers. "Gathering strength for his next big bounce, more like!"

Chapter Two

"Come along, Bob," Amy said. "Time for you to meet the outside world!"

It was the following morning, and Amy had hardly been able to sleep, with a lively Bob racing around her room for most of the night.

She opened the back door wide. "Look, Bob!" she went on. "Grass, trees, and lots of different things to play with.

You don't have to just sit indoors staring at everything anymore.

For the past four weeks Bob had often sat at the window, paws up against the glass, gazing out. Now he could actually get out there. Amy could hardly wait to see what he was going to do.

Bob was sitting on a kitchen chair, giving himself a bath. Seeing the open door, he bounced down and came to stand in the open doorway.

His nostrils twitched as he sniffed the fresh air. then his ears quivered as they picked up outdoor noises that were new and strange to him.

He looked up at Amy, his green eyes

big and wide. "Can I go out there now?" he meowed.

"Don't be nervous, Bob," Amy said gently. "It's lovely outside. There's grass and bushes and a big tree and—"

"What are we waiting for, then?" Bob meowed loudly and, before Amy

could say any more, he took off.

Amy ran after Bob as he bounded down the path, then plunged into the grass.

When he reached the end of the lawn and hit the cool earth of the flower bed, Bob stopped. "Wow!" he meowed. "This playground is just great!"

Bob bounced around the garden for some time, jumping at flies, playing hide-and-seek with Amy in the long grass, and pouncing on things.

Suddenly, Bob spotted Georgina, Mrs.-Neil-next-door's big gray cat. Georgina was stretched out on the roof of her owner's little garden shed, next to the fence.

Bob ran over to the shed and looked

up at Georgina. Then he looked back at Amy. "I'm going up to make friends!" he meowed.

"I wouldn't climb up there, Bob," Amy warned. "Georgina is a very grown-up cat. She might not like bouncy kittens, and—"

But Bob didn't wait to hear the rest. Digging his claws into the rough wood of the fence, he scampered up, then jumped onto the shed roof, next to Georgina.

The old gray cat opened one eye and looked lazily at the ball of ginger fluff that had suddenly appeared next to her.

Bob looked back at her. "Hello," he mewed. "I live in the house next door."

Georgina just kept on looking at him with one eye.

"Anyway," Bob went on, "would you like to play a game of 'pounce the mouse'?" He jumped back and forth to demonstrate.

Georgina opened her other eye. Her

tail began to swish from side to side. "Watch it, or I'll pounce on you," she meowed, sounding a little annoyed.

"I think you'd better come down, Bob," Amy called, seeing that the old cat was looking angry. "I don't think Georgina likes kittens."

But Bob didn't listen. "Oh, come on!" he meowed to Georgina. "It'll be fun!" To get her in the mood, he bounced right up to Georgina and pounced on her swaying tail.

Hissing loudly, Georgina sprang to her feet, ears flattened and fur bristling. Suddenly she seemed twice her size.

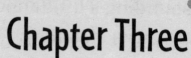

Chapter Three

Bob shrank back, startled. "Sorry," he meowed weakly. "Didn't mean to offend you." He waited a moment, then crept closer again. "Perhaps another time—"

Georgina began to make a funny growling sound in the back of her throat. But *still* Bob didn't take the hint. She gave him a sideswipe with her paw. "Go away!" she hissed.

"Bob!" Amy called. "Come down *now*! Georgina doesn't want to play."

Just then, Mrs. Neil came out into her yard to hang out her laundry. "You've got your new kitten out here!" she said, putting down the basket. "Oh, isn't he gorgeous?"

Amy nodded proudly. "It's his first day in the big world. He's just introduced himself to your Georgina, but I don't think she was too keen. She gave him a bop on the ear."

Mrs. Neil grinned. "Georgina is an old lady now, like me. She likes to keep naughty little boys like Bob in check." Mrs. Neil put down her laundry basket and said, "Can I take the little guy down for a cuddle?"

Amy smiled. "'Course you can."

Watched by a disapproving Georgina, Mrs. Neil reached up and lifted Bob from the shed room. "He's a darling!" she said, stroking Bob and tickling him under the chin.

Bob wriggled out of Mrs. Neil's arms and ran onto her shoulders to settle himself around the back of her neck. Mrs. Neil laughed. "Oh, they're lovely when they're this young," she said. "I sometimes wish they could stay this small and cute forever."

"They're so naughty, though," Amy said. She told Mrs. Neil about some of the things that Bob had been up to, like hanging on the curtains, drinking the bathwater, and licking butter out of the dish. "And half of those my mother doesn't even know about!" she finished.

Mrs. Neil nodded. "Yes, now that you mention it, I remember Georgina doing the same thing. Maybe it's just as well that they do grow up, then," she said.

Bob decided that he was bored with all this chat. He took a flying leap from Mrs. Neil's shoulders and landed on a fence post. Then he dropped back into his own yard. They watched him springing like a hare over the lawn.

"Off he goes," Mrs. Neil said. "He sure is a little spitfire!"

Bob ran right down to the bottom of the yard and, without hesitating, shinned straight up the big oak tree in the corner.

"They love climbing trees," Mrs. Neil said. "And it's good for their claws, too. It sharpens them, you know."

"It's a huge tree, though," Amy said, frowning worriedly. "I hope he doesn't get stuck up there."

They watched as Bob rounded the trunk of the tree and began to skitter and scratch his way out onto a branch.

"Kittens are quite clever," Mrs. Neil said. "They don't usually go anywhere they can't get down from."

Just as she said that, they saw Bob stop and look all around him. He began to meow loudly.

"Oh! He's stuck!" Amy said. "I knew it!" She ran over to the tree.

Bob stared down at her. "This is soooo exciting," he purred. "I can see into all the other yards from here!"

"What if he really can't get down?" Amy cried.

Mrs. Neil tutted anxiously, watching Bob. Then she said, "I've got an idea. It used to work with Georgina when she wouldn't come in—" She went into her house and reappeared a few minutes later with a box of cat biscuits.

"I'm going to stay up here forever," Bob meowed.

"He hasn't moved at all," Amy said. "I think he's scared of falling off."

"Let's see if this works," Mrs. Neil said, pushing open her gate. She strode into Amy's yard, shaking the box of cat treats.

Bob recognized the sound. Food!

Mrs. Neil shook again. "Here, puss-puss-puss!" she said.

"Purreoww!" Georgina, on hearing the familiar noise, had jumped down from the shed and was sitting at Mrs. Neil's feet, looking expectantly up at the box.

"Yes, there's some for you as well," Mrs. Neil said, and she bent and poured out a few biscuits for Georgina.

"Shake it again, Mrs. Neil," Amy said. "Bob heard you shaking it, too!"

As the box was shaken again, Bob changed his mind about staying up in the tree forever. His tummy was rumbling. As much as he liked climbing trees, he decided that he liked biscuits better.

Carefully, he managed to turn on the branch. "Phew!" That was a little tricky!" he mewed.

"He's coming down! Hurrah!" Amy said as Bob edged back to the main trunk of the tree, then scampered down it. "I thought I was going to have to call the fire department," she told Bob as he munched on his treats.

"Let's hope he's learned not to go where he shouldn't," Mrs. Neil said, smiling.

"Yes, Bob," Amy agreed. "No more climbing dangerous trees, okay?"

Bob didn't seem to hear her. And as soon as he'd finished his biscuits, he took off again like a small ginger rocket, racing up the yard and into the kitchen.

Amy stayed talking to Mrs. Neil for a while, stroking Georgina, who seemed in a much better mood now that the silly young kitten had gone away.

Suddenly there was a short scream from inside. "Amy!" Mrs. Myers shouted. "Come and get your kitten out of this mixing bowl *immediately!*"

"Oops!" said Amy.

"Maybe he hasn't *quite* learned his lesson," said Mrs. Neil.

Chapter Four

Two days later, Amy stood at the foot of the big oak tree, staring up. "Not again, Bob!" she said. Through the leaves and branches she could just see a trace of gingery fur. It was only a glimpse, though, because Bob was a long way up.

"Come on, Bob!" she called. "Puss-puss-puss!"

Through the greenery came a faint meow. "Not just yet, Amy—"

"Bob-Bob-Bob!" Amy called. "Come on down, boy!"

The meow was a little louder this time. "Not just *yet*, Amy. I'm busy!"

Amy sighed worriedly. Bob seemed to

be stuck again. He had been going into the backyard for three days now, but instead of the big outdoors using up his energy, it seemed to make him bouncier than ever. He was still always getting into mischief.

She went back inside the house and brought out a box of cat treats. "Bob-Bob-Bob!" she called "Lovely rabbit-flavored biscuits!" She shook the box briskly.

Bob stopped examining the old empty bird's nest he'd found on one of the branches. *Mmm, I could do with a snack*, he thought. It had been quite a hectic morning.

"Coming!" he meowed.

He made his way back down the tree,

arriving with a scrabble and a bounce at the bottom.

"Oh, thank goodness!" Amy tipped some biscuits onto the ground. "Bob, I do wish you wouldn't keep climbing trees. I'm always frightened you won't be able to get back down."

Insulted, Bob pretended not to hear that. *I could get down from* any *tree*, he thought with a huff.

The very next day, Bob was in disgrace. Mrs. Myers had been making cheese sandwiches for lunch. Bob had decided that he would like a cheese sandwich, too. He'd bounced onto the kitchen to help himself. Luckily, Amy's mother had been looking in the fridge at the time. Amy had put Bob back on the floor right away.

But Bob wasn't put off so easily.

He'd bounced onto the table again, and this time Mrs. Myers had seen Bob up there herself. Now he was in big trouble.

Amy sat picking miserably at her sandwich. Bob was outside, meowing away and scratching at the back door. "Can Bob come in again now?" Amy asked.

"No," Mrs. Myers said. "He's got to learn his lesson."

Just then, two gingery-white tufty ears appeared in the glass panel of the back door. "Oh, look!" Amy cried. "Bob's standing on his hind legs to try to look in. Oh, Mom, isn't he sweet?"

"Sweet—and very naughty," her mother said. But Amy could see she was smiling a little.

Amy took the dirty plates to the sink. "Can I go out to him, please?"

Her mother nodded, then said, "I suppose I'll have to eat all the banana custard myself—"

Amy loved banana custard.

"Well . . . I'm sure Bob will be okay on his own for just a bit longer."

Chapter Five

Bob's cute pose at the back door hadn't worked. Mrs. Myers *still* hadn't let him come back in.

He looked around for something to cheer him up. The oak tree! He meowed one last time at the back door, then raced across the lawn.

In seconds, he was bouncing from one large, leafy branch to another, chasing after sparrows. But they soon all flew away.

Bob swatted some tiny insects that were scurrying along the branch. He loved it up here. The branch swayed up and down as a light breeze ruffled its leaves.

The kitten looked around him. He could see for miles! He could see that snobby cat Georgina on the patio next door. And a black tomcat peering over the garden wall two doors down.

And then Bob saw something else. Something quite frightening. "Oh, no!" he meowed. "I need to get help!"

Amy scraped her pudding bowl clean. Bob had stopped scratching at the door.

She went out into the yard to find him, but she couldn't see him anywhere. Frowning, she went right down to the bushes at the bottom, calling as she went, but she still couldn't see him. She searched in the shed, but he wasn't there, either.

There was no sign of Bob anywhere. Unless . . . Amy walked over to the foot of the old oak tree and looked up. "Bob?" she called.

Faintly, from far up in the tree, she heard an answering meow.

"Oh, not again!" Sighing, she trudged back indoors to get the box of cat treats.

"Bob-Bob-Bob!" Amy called a few seconds later. She rattled the biscuit box hard. "Come on, boy! Biscuits!"

Amy called and called, and shook and shook. The meowing continued. And to Amy, it seemed to get louder and louder. But there was no rustle from the leaves to tell her that Bob was making his way down.

"You must *really* be stuck this time, Bob," Amy muttered worriedly. She went indoors to see if her mom would call the fire department.

Mrs. Myers was upstairs in the spare room, working at her computer. "Don't be silly!" she said when Amy told her the story. "You can't expect the fire department to come out just because a kitten's been up a tree for a few minutes."

"It's not just a few minutes," Amy said. "It's been almost half an hour now. What if he falls?"

Mrs. Myers shook her head. "Left to their own devices, kittens will always come down trees by themselves," she said. "You've just got to leave him to it. Do something else and forget about him for a while!"

She pressed a key, and her printer started to whirr. "I really have to work, Amy. That kitten gets quite enough attention from you without fussing around him. He'll come down when he's good and ready."

Amy sighed. She went downstairs and out to the oak tree. Halfheartedly she rattled the biscuit box and called Bob once more, but with no luck. Bob's meowing was becoming quite frantic now. Amy was sure he was scared to pieces.

Suddenly Amy's eyes fell on the old

wooden ladder that was propped up against the wall at the bottom of the garden.

She went over to the ladder and tried to pull it away from the wall. It was very heavy. Amy heaved again, holding the highest rungs she could reach.

Slowly, the top of the ladder came away from the wall. With all her strength, she dragged it toward the oak tree and let go. Amy held her breath.

Yes! The ladder landed with a clatter against the thick trunk. Pleased with herself, Amy pushed it firmly into position. It seemed safe and secure.

"I'm coming, Bob!" she called, putting a foot on the first rung.

There was an answering meow. "Hurry, Amy!" Bob called.

As she climbed higher, Amy could see a tiny gingery face looking down at her through the branches. The ladder wobbled slightly, and she stopped and held on to a branch. It was a little scary. She didn't want to look down.

Bob gave another long, drawn-out me-ooow! "Come up and see what I can see!"

"Yes, I know you're scared," Amy said. "I am, too. But I'm coming for you, now." Glancing over into Mrs. Neil's yard, she saw Georgina pacing up and down outside Mrs. Neil's greenhouse. *That's weird*, Amy thought. She climbed

up another two rungs of the ladder.

Bob watched her intently, his green eyes alert. "Look again, Amy!" he mewed.

And then Amy's eyes opened wide. She could see Mrs. Neil lying on the greenhouse floor. "Mrs. Neil!" she cried. "Are you all right, Mrs. Neil?"

There was no reply. Amy gasped and leaned over to get a better look. Mrs. Neil was very still. What on earth was wrong? Was she really badly hurt?

Amy began to feel frightened. "Mrs. Neil!" she called again. "Oh, Mrs. Neil!"

"That's what I wanted to show you!" meowed Bob from farther up the tree.

Amy glanced up. "You'll have to wait, Bob," she said. "I've got to tell Mom!" And she scrambled down the ladder as quickly as she could.

Chapter Six

"Mom! Mom! Come quickly!" Amy shouted, running up the stairs two at a time. "Mom!"

As Amy burst through the door of Mrs. Myers's office, she saw her mother was on the phone.

"Excuse me one moment," Mrs. Myers said very politely into the phone. Then she put her hand over the receiver and turned to Amy. "What is it, Amy?" she asked in a rather angry voice.

"You've got to come down, Mom!" Amy cried.

Mrs. Myers sighed. "It's not that kitten again, is it? What's he done now?"

Amy shook her head. "It's not Bob," she said, hopping from foot to foot. "It's Mrs. Neil! She's out in her greenhouse and she's fallen on the floor. Her leg's all funny—and she's not moving or talking to me!"

Mrs. Myers stood up quickly and spoke into the receiver. "I'm so sorry, it's a domestic emergency. May I call you back?" She put the phone down. "Let's go!"

Mrs. Myers followed Amy back down

the stairs. "But how on earth did you come to see Mrs. Neil in her green house?" she asked as they ran.

"I was . . . er . . . climbing the ladder," Amy said.

"Amy! You know you shouldn't have done that without asking!" her mother said.

"I had to!" Amy pleaded. "Bob was really and truly stuck. I mean, he still is!"

"Well and truly stuck, huh?" repeated her mother as they ran through the kitchen. "Who's that, then?"

There, in the kitchen, nose in her bowl and crunching cat treats for all he was worth, was Bob.

"Oh!" Amy cried.

As her mother disappeared out of the kitchen door, Amy swooped on Bob, picked him up, and hugged him. "You got down on your own again, you pest of a kitten!"

"Of course I did!" Bob purred. "Don't I always?"

Carrying Bob, Amy ran out into the yard. Her mother called over the fence and told her to dial 911 and ask for an ambulance to come right away.

Still holding Bob tightly, Amy turned and ran back into the house. Oh, she hoped Mrs. Neil would be all right!

Twenty minutes later, the ambulance arrived.

"I felt dizzy," Mrs. Neil told the ambulance crew. "I don't remember anything else until I heard the ambulance siren outside. . . ."

Mrs. Neil was weak and shaken up after her fall. She had to go to the hospital to have X rays taken of her injured leg to see if it was broken.

Bob sat perfectly still in Amy's arms, watching as Mrs. Neil was lifted onto a stretcher.

Mrs. Neil beckoned Amy over to her. "Thank you so much, my dear," she said in a very faint voice. "I don't know how long I'd have been lying here if you hadn't seen me."

"That's okay," Amy said shyly.

"I helped, too!" Bob purred. But no one seemed to notice.

"Yes, you did well, honey," the ambulance woman said to Amy, placing a soft, red blanket around Mrs. Neil. "It was a good thing you were up that ladder."

Amy's mother nodded. "But you shouldn't really use that ladder on your own again, young lady," she added sternly. Then she smiled and gave Amy a quick hug.

Bob meowed loudly. "What about me?"

Holding Bob with one arm, Amy hugged her mother back. Then she looked down at her kitten. "We ought to thank Bob, really," she said.

"Who's Bob?" asked the ambulance woman. "Your brother?"

"No, this is Bob," Amy said, holding up her kitten. "If he hadn't got stuck up the oak tree, I never would have climbed the ladder and seen Mrs. Neil lying on the floor."

Bob gave a purry meow. "It wasn't *quite* like that, Amy. I *wasn't* stuck!"

"Then I'm very grateful to Bob, too!" Mrs. Neil said shakily as the ambulance crew carried her over to the ambulance. "I could have been on that floor all night—and who knows what might have become of me! When I get back, I'll buy Bob a big bag of cat treats to say thank you."

Bob sat in Amy's arms and purred. They'd gotten it slightly wrong, but at least everyone knew now that he'd had a part in the rescue. And a big bag of cat treats sounded pretty good to him!

Just as Mrs. Neil was being lifted into the ambulance, Bob wriggled out of

Amy's arms. He leaped onto the hedge to have a good look around.

"I'm watching you, Bob!" Amy called to him warningly.

Bob pretended not to hear. "Bye, Mrs. Neil!" he meowed. "Hope you're all right! You don't mind if I give your apple tree a try, do you?" Then he bounded down onto the lawn—and found himself face-to-face with Georgina.

Bob bounced back a few paces in alarm. Last time he'd been this close to Georgina, she'd given him a nasty swipe.

But this time she was purring, so he plonked himself down next to her and started to purr, too.

"Feel free! Anyone who rescues my Mrs. Neil is a friend of mine. And though I'm a bit old to do much climbing myself now, I can recommend the lilac tree and the pear tree, too."

"Thanks!" squeaked Bob, hardly able

to believe his luck. In a blur of ginger fur, he zipped across the lawn and shinned straight up the apple tree.

"Oh, good heavens!" said Mrs. Neil, who had seen Bob through the open ambulance doors.

"There he goes again!" Apples fell to the ground as Bob scampered to the top of the tree.

"Time for another rescue?" the ambulance woman said, smiling.

Amy shook her head. "Now I *know* Bob can get down by himself." Then she frowned and turned to Mrs. Neil. "But if Bob wasn't stuck up the oak tree, Mrs. Neil, why didn't he come down for biscuits like he usually does?"

Mrs. Neil shook her head. "Very unusual," she said.

Amy smiled. "I think he saw that you had fallen and wanted me to climb up and see you, too."

Everyone laughed.

"That's a good one!" said the ambulance man.

"Don't be silly, honey!" said Amy's mother.

"It's a nice thought, though," said Mrs. Neil.

Bob meowed happily as he swayed in the branches at the top of the apple tree.

Mrs. Neil's leg was very sore from her fall, but luckily it wasn't broken. Apart from some nasty bruises, the old lady

from some nasty bruises, the old lady seemed fine. But from then on, Bob always kept an eye on her—whenever he was bouncing up trees.

If you like horses, friends, fun, and excitement, then you'll love

Sheltie

The little pony with the big heart!

written and illustrated by Peter Clover

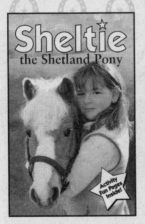

JOIN SHELTIE AND EMMA IN THEIR MANY THRILLING ADVENTURES TOGETHER!

#1 Sheltie the Shetland Pony
0-689-83574-4/$3.99

#2 Sheltie Saves the Day!
0-689-83575-2/$3.99

#3 Sheltie and the Runaway
0-689-83576-0/$3.99

#4 Sheltie Finds a Friend
0-689-83975-8/$3.99

#5 Sheltie to the Rescue
0-689-83976-6/$3.99

#6 Sheltie in Danger
0-689-84028-4/$3.99

Aladdin Paperbacks • Simon & Schuster Children's Publishing
www.SimonSaysKids.com

Everyone needs Puppy Friends!

Bouncy and cute, furry and huggable, what could be more perfect than a puppy?

written and illustrated by
Jenny Dale

#1 Gus the Greedy Puppy
0-689-83423-3 $3.99

#2 Lily the Lost Puppy
0-689-83404-7 $3.99

#3 Spot the Sporty Puppy
0-689-83424-1 $3.99

#4 Lenny the Lazy Puppy
0-689-83552-3 $3.99

#5 Max the Muddy Puppy
0-689-83553-1 $3.99

#6 Billy the Brave Puppy
0-689-83554-X $3.99

#7 Nipper the Noisy Puppy
0-689-83974-X $3.99

ALADDIN PAPERBACKS
Simon & Schuster Children's Publishing
www.SimonSaysKids.com